Where The Sea Meets The Sky

M.L. Kasper

www.trafford.com

North America & international
toll-free: 1 888 232 4444 (USA & Canada)
phone: 250 383 6864 ✦ fax: 250 383 6804
email: info@trafford.com

The United Kingdom & Europe
phone: +44 (0)1865 722 113 ✦ local rate: 0845 230 9601
facsimile: +44 (0)1865 722 868 ✦ email: info.uk@trafford.com

10 9 8 7 6 5 4 3 2

Prologue

A bright moon-shadow follows a slight man with a goatee as he struggles to load a large number of small wooden boxes into the dinghy. The ebb tide of life is pulling him into a state of decline.

He stops his work and turns toward a building. His eyes pierce the night like red cosmic beams. In the building is a riddled mess of broken picture frames and smashed pieces of model ships spread among broken glass.

Moonlight rides the incoming sea as it leaks around a nearby scuttled ship. The name *Lady Royal* is barely visible, even though the lunar light lends a brightness rivaling daylight.

In his haste, a box catches the side of the rowboat and is smashed by its collision with a small rock outcropping. A section of wood separates, revealing broken glass. The moonlight catches numerous muted-gold globs embedded in a waxy mass.

Awaiting the rowboat is a tug—anchored and fully stocked. The ship's safe is open and more wooden boxes fill it. Stacked next to it are several more.

Rearranging her red hair, a tall and slender woman abruptly turns her head; she hears the bearded man secure the dinghy to the tug. She hurries to the side railings to assist. More wooden boxes are handed from the man on the dinghy to the tall woman. As the last box is handed off, the man climbs aboard and the two embrace.

"I've destroyed the last of it. It's not ours anymore. The bloody court gave it away to the others ... the infidels! At least we have the gold. That should give us a new start."

The tug was soon under way and pushed through the water. A funnel of moonlight stretched across the flat sea directly to the pilot-house window. Numerous charts were scattered about, but there was no need for these, for the man with the goatee and the angry eyes had navigated these waters many times and was well aware of what to expect. What he couldn't know was what awaited him at his first port of call—Seattle. There, he and his tall, redheaded companion planned to join what remained of his faithful followers. They would make their way to San Francisco.

It was April of 1933, and he wondered if he had it in him to start over again.

Once Upon An Island

Alone white Lexus with New York license plates descended the Sea to Sky Highway en route to Horseshoe Bay. On the back seat was a week-old copy of the *Wall Street Journal*. The front bumper and grill were encrusted with insects—the kind you find in Saskatchewan.

Nick tightened his grip on the leather steering wheel while glancing at his watch.

"Are we going to make this ferry, Nick?"

"You bet," Nick replied.

Sara pressed her feet hard into the floor carpet as the car slowed to join the lineup of various vehicles already being swallowed by the open doors of the ferry. In short time the ferry doors closed and large numbers of people swarmed the decks and passageways in preparation for their journey.

Nick and Sara Konic crossed the deck, grabbing onto the railings. A powerful yet muffled blast from the ferry's whistle announced "all was ready" and motion imminent. Nick's legs tensed as the ship pulled away from the dock.

The couple felt a "casting off" of the past as they watched Horseshoe Bay become smaller. Majestic, snow-capped, cloud-piercing mountains that rose from the ocean floor now defined the enormity of the present.

Sara tilted her head back and her lung's expanded as the sea breeze entered, filling her nostrils with a fresh and familiar scent. The moist, briny smell of the sea reminded her of her childhood years enjoying summer vacations on her uncle's fishing boats.

Nick reached for Sara's hand as the couple glanced out over an archipelago of small islands to an eternity of sky and water.

"This is what we are going to see every day for the rest of our retired lives," said Nick.

"It's breathtaking," replied Sara.

"How many islands do you suppose there are?" Sara asked. Her voice exuded excitement and lively curiosity.

"You're the "daughter of Canada" who was born and raised here, Sara, I should be asking *you*. I'm just the New Yorker who got seduced by two beauties ... you and British Columbia."

"Seduced, huh?"

"You know it."

"Nick, do you realize that by living the past twenty years in New York with you, I've lived in New York almost as long as in B.C.?"

"Which do you feel more like, Sara?"

"Wherever you are feels like home to me."

Sara's response caused Nick to turn and look into her eyes with a schoolboy smile.

"Now, Nick, you haven't answered my question."

"What question, Sara?"

"Nick ... how many islands *do* you think are here?"

"I'm not sure. The realtor did say there were over three-hundred privately owned islands in addition to those that the Crown, as well as the Ministry of Defense, claim jurisdiction over. And that doesn't include those north of Vancouver Island where the Queen Charlottes lie."

"That sounds like an awful lot of islands. I can't wait to see all of them and what's on each one," Sara continued.

"Shall we go inside and grab a good seat?" Nick asked.

"Yes, a window seat with a view would be nice. I can't believe how tired I feel."

The ferry continued to slice through the water like a majestic ocean liner while the tired couple settled into their seats by the window. As Nick glanced out he got lost in a semi-dream. Was it only last night, he thought, that he and Sara celebrated over king crab and champagne toasts? They had crossed the New York–Canada border in Ontario and had pushed through some pretty long driving days. Nick had convinced Sara that an overnight in Whistler was deserved. After all, it *was* their anniversary and the beginning of retired life in their newly purchased home on Vancouver Island.

Nick rubbed his eyes and yawned as his mind returned to the present. What would the future hold for him and Sara, and what island adventures awaited them? Life would change, he felt, as certain as the seascape he was now viewing.

++++++++++++++

Nick and Sara quickly adapted to life in their seaside cottage with the type of excitement and joy usually reserved for newlyweds. Within a short time a new sense of balance and routine entered their lives. The days were no longer measured by the passing of their given weekday names as Nick and Sara had little need to differentiate a Wednesday from a Thursday. In addition to being on "Retired Time," they were introduced to something well-known by the Islanders as "Island Time." Island Time became part of Nick and Sara's lifestyle. A relaxed state of affairs ensued, and they soon felt that a certain minimal relationship—expressed in terms of time—must exist between people conducting any sort of business or conversation. The ties to this concept were ever-present throughout the islands.

Unmeasured days slipped into barely measurable months. Nick soon found opportunities to visit the local town, looking for familiar places with new names. The Book Bank had become his favorite local antiquarian bookshop. Its walls of imagined treasure bound in boards of cloth and leather called to him and excited his sense of the unknown. Today, having dropped Sara off at a local eatery where she was to meet with her old high school girlfriends for lunch, translated into an opportunity for Nick to call on the Book Bank.

Nick had met Fran Neilson on earlier visits and enjoyed the delightful conversation she offered. Fran was left the business when her husband Olie finally closed the last chapter of his life's story. Fran and Olie had located the bookshop in what was formerly a bank building, and it seemed apropos that tomes now garnished such a building. The main vault housed the rare and more exotic books, and was the first section Nick sought out when calling on this bookshop.

Nick stood beside Fran as she turned the flat, heavy-looking bronze key and gave the day gate a swing, allowing him access to what now served as the rare books room. The gate swung shut behind him with a finality that reminded him that this area was of limited access. Nick was enjoying the soothing music of Nora Jones that was being piped into the room as he walked across the oriental rugs to reach for a leather-bound book. He was amongst the highest caliber of friends. They came in all sizes and bindings, and all had a story to tell. Nick knew that Fran was familiar with all the books in the rare book section and was totally versed in the tales and local history each contained.

Nick's mind now turned to Fran as he restored a copy of *Mayne's British Columbia* to its shelf. He wondered if she might not be an excellent resource person to get him up to speed with his new surroundings. Having returned to the front counter, Nick waited patiently for Fran to finish with a customer.

"May I help you, Nick?"

Nick noticed Fran's striking image and made a conscious effort not to let his eyes reveal his thoughts. Fran's silvery blond hair was drawn up in a tight bun; her erect posture completed the clean, smooth line of her profile. She broke into a warm smile as she waited for Nick's response.

"Why, yes ... thank you. I'm looking for something written by a local author that would be light reading. Maybe a novel or a collection of short stories would do. No history though. I'm not looking to be informed today ... just entertained."

In less than a minute Fran had a small selection of books for Nick to peruse.

Grabbing an old-looking book with a tattered dusk jacket, Nick now turned his wrist and glanced at the black face of his Rado watch. He realized he'd better get hopping if he wasn't going to be late picking up Sara. Even though he and Sara lived on Island Time they were still punctual with their mutual appointments. Nick opened the book he selected and took a quick look at the price written in pencil. Closing the cover, Nick peered at the dust jacket. The words *Poor Man's Rock* were faint and partial.

"What's the damage, Fran?"

"That'll be twenty dollars, Nick. I think you're going to enjoy this book."

The Harbor at Nanaimo

The sounds made by fishing boats docking and the screeching of seagulls were temporarily overpowered by those of a landing float plane. Commuters disembarked and contributed to the wharf activities. Blocks away, the time displayed on the watchtower clock could be easily seen announcing an advanced stage of the day's predictable journey. Soon the harbor would return to a less busy, quieter song.

Not far away, barely beyond the sound of lapping waves and below the glide of a single gull, a companionless, unkempt man, whose grooming was not only neglected but close to non-existent, was exerting an enormous effort just to negotiate the sidewalk. He seemed to be arguing with some imagined adversary. He was, no doubt, a soul occupying a body that had tested the rougher side of life's offerings.

As he crossed the street and slowly managed his way down the next block, a pickup appeared. The yellow Ford looked out of place because it was fairly new and shiny. It parked in front of a run-down building that displayed the word *Pawnshop*. This word seemed to have been more the result of some graffiti prank than any serious effort to convey that a legitimate business existed there.

Inside the pickup were Nick and Sara.

"I think we should forget this and check with the local locksmith shop, Nick," Sara suggested. "Just look at that man on the next block—he looks dangerous."

Nick quickly reassured Sara that the unkempt man wearing a pea jacket and toque was probably just an old "Sea Dog."

"Nevertheless," Sara said with some trepidation, "he looks like he could be trouble. Just look! He can barely stand upright. This part of town is next to the Reservation and it is not what I would consider safe," Sara continued to protest. "Lots of fights use to break out in this part of town when I was a kid," she recalled.

Nick noted that the streets were now empty and felt that Sara's concern was really unfounded.

"Listen, Sara, I'm sure the truck will be okay here. We've already been to the only other two pawnshops in town and one of these has *got* to have an old safe to sell. I just know I'll find one for the house, and if not here, then I'll take your advice and our next stop will be the locksmith shop."

Sara sighed. "Well … I guess so. After all, we

have to get this truck back to my brother. He was nice enough to let us borrow it, and I don't think we should tie it up all day."

"You're right, Sara," said Nick as he slid out and locked the door, feeling for the first time in ages the pressure of a time constraint. I'm not in New York anymore, Nick thought, as he and Sara were about to enter the pawnshop. So why do I feel rushed and anxious?

The interior of the pawnshop offered Sara no more comfort than its facade. Nick made his way past table tops and broken-down display cases filled with power tools, CDs, DVDs, and an assortment of hunting knives. On the walls were wood carvings—supposedly done by the local First Nations people.

Nick planted his foot to do a 180-degree turn when his attention was drawn to what was obviously no ordinary piece of furniture. It was partially draped by a soiled Hudson Bay blanket, affording a view with a promise. A brass handle and the lower half of what appeared to be an elaborate nameplate were clearly visible—inviting him to lift the old blanket.

"Can I help you with anything?" a voice blurted out.

Nick was abrubtly snapped back to the present by the words he had heard behind him. He turned slightly to see the source of the request.

Standing near, with one hand on a display case, was a young man who seemed timid and totally out of place.

"Is this a safe?" Nick asked the storekeeper.

"Why, yes," was the young man's response. "But it doesn't work. I know that for a fact. I asked the owner that question when I first started working here and was told that it's been here forever and nobody knows how to open it."

"Is it for sale?" Nick asked.

"Holy jeez, I don't know."

"Well," Nick continued, "if it's not the store safe … then it must be for sale if it's out here."

"Well, I suppose it *is* for sale, but I haven't worked here very long and don't know that for sure *or* what it would sell for." The storekeeper's response noticeably lacked confidence.

Nick made another effort to determine the safe's status. "It wouldn't be out here … I would think it would be in the back if it wasn't for sale."

Nick looked the safe over carefully as he removed the blanket; he noticed the name Chubb. He immediately sensed value in it remembering that back in New York his friend Alex, who was in the safe trade, once told him that a Chubb was the Rolls Royce of safes. It was a rather small safe and quite like what he had hoped to find. Nick glanced at Sara, seeking her reassurance for what he was about to do. He offered the young man one hundred dollars in cash. It was a starting point, because although he felt this a good safe, it would certainly require a very expensive opening fee by a professional. Perhaps in the opening process it might have to be destroyed—and it might not even be repairable.

The young storekeeper kept silent, although he

seemed to be in agreement with Nick's offer as he continued to nod his head.

Nick made a last effort to close the negotiation, still uncertain if he was getting a fantastic deal or throwing away what money he was offering. "Well, can you call the owner and ask?"

"That's not possible because he's gone up-island fishing and I know, for a fact, he is out of range for his cell phone."

"Well," Nick continued, "I have to know one way or the other because after I walk out of this shop, I'm heading to the locksmith shop, and I'll certainly buy one of theirs if I don't get this."

"There's only one locksmith shop in town, and you'll pay them a lot more than that. They only have new safes in there and they are pricey," the young man informed Nick in a voice that now betrayed a hint of "attitude."

Nick felt he would leave it to destiny with a final offer. If turned down, he promised himself to walk away from this.

"Last offer—a buck and a half and no paper. I would think that your boss would be glad to be rid of something he can't use and still pick up good cash."

"Deal!" the young man blurted out with a sudden burst of newfound confidence and excitement.

"I have a cart in the truck along with a couple of planks," Nick said with satisfaction. "Would you mind giving me a hand?"

A sense of relief swept over them all, and with the negotiations completed, what had turned into a chore was finally over.

Nick loaded the newly purchased safe onto the truck, then slamming the tailgate shut, he walked around to the driver's door. Sara had been waiting in the cab of the pickup during the loading of the safe. As Nick entered the truck, he felt an apprehension that caused him to wonder if the deal he had just completed was somehow responsible for this eerie feeling. Sliding across the seat and closing the driver's door, Nick turned to Sara and became startled.

"What's wrong honey?" Nick inquired, not knowing if he really wanted an answer.

Sara was not herself; she looked uneasy. "Didn't you see that bizarre-looking lady who was standing by the pawnshop window?"

"I didn't see anyone," Nick replied.

"While you were loading the safe I saw a woman in a long, black dress."

"What was so special about her?"

"I don't know, Nick. It's just that she looked, by her dress and appearance, as if she were from a different time period or something. She also had a stern stare that made me uneasy."

"Well, where is she now?"

"That's just it, she was only there for a second or two. I was distracted by a seagull, and when I turned back, it was as if she had never been there. It was all so quick, I don't know … maybe I imagined the whole thing. It *is* getting dark out, Nick, and she *was* only there a second or two."

"Honey, I think we're getting overtired, and your eyes are in need of a rest. Let's go home so I can get this pickup back to your brother Don."

The Safe

Nick leaned back in his swivel chair. He looked across the cherrywood floor at a wall of immense windows. Oversized wooden uprights supported a massive lam beam. The materials were constructed in such a way that the natural world was drawn from the outside into the living area. Nick had long forgotten about the oversized, white Starbucks cup, still full of green tea. On the computer, the stock market web page had reverted to a screensaver, and on TV, the *Report On Business*, or *ROB* show, was going unnoticed. The world of business was relegated to secondary status as Nick's attention was drawn beyond the sixty kilometers of ocean to the distant snow-capped mountains on the mainland. A gathering of dark clouds had accumulated. Behind the clouds the sun's rays formed a cartwheel of bright spokes.

The spell Nick was enjoying suddenly ended when he heard a vehicle door closing. He knew the locksmith had finally arrived. Soon it would be known if his negotiating at the pawnshop was worth such an involved effort.

Sara greeted the locksmith, and soon they were all downstairs viewing the spoils of Nick's bartering. Both Sara and Nick waited anxiously while the neatly groomed lock mechanic inspected their newly acquired safe.

"Wow," he uttered. "English—and super well made. I don't suppose there is *any* chance of finding the keys for this?"

"That's why you're here," said Nick in a kind voice that expressed confidence in the locksmith.

The locksmith shook his head and puckered his lips as if about to say something not easily said.

"We don't ever see these," he volunteered. "You might get to see the occasional one in Vancouver, but not ever on the island."

"What's the verdict?" Nick asked with some apprehension.

"Well, this is not an opening I would feel comfortable with. You won't find anyone locally who would be well versed in this type of container, especially one that is protected by *two* key-operated Chubb locks."

"Yes," interrupted Sara, "I was wondering why there wasn't a combination dial. Don't all safes have combination dials?"

"Well," replied the locksmith, "in Europe the key-operated lock is actually the preferred system. On older

English safes, like we have here, your chances of finding a key lock over a combination are even greater. I'd say this safe probably dates around the 1930s or 1940s vintage. The second key lock would also indicate it was made with a high level of security in mind, or maybe even a commercial application where dual custody is required. You see," he continued, "these types of safes are protected on all six sides. That is to say, the bottom, top and sides are as difficult to achieve an opening on as the door. An opening on these sides with a hole big enough to get a hand through isn't going to happen either! Did this container come off a ship?" the locksmith inquired.

"I don't know the history regarding it," Nick offered, "only that it's old … and locked. You might say it's something I acquired as a curiosity."

The locksmith now made Nick an offer.

"I could try to open it if damage is not a concern and you weren't planning on reusing it."

"What the hell good is that?" Nick erupted, losing his composure for a moment.

"Well, at least you'll know if there is anything in it," the locksmith snapped back.

"*Anything in it?*" Nick replied in complete shock. "I never even thought about that. I don't think the previous owner would have sold it to me if he thought there was a chance that something was in it."

"Yeah," agreed the locksmith. "Usually the owner knows if the safe is holding anything of value. That information usually follows the safe from owner to owner, unless it was passed on through an inheritance, or if the owner kept it a secret and took it to the grave with him. In cases like this, the only thing we usually find, on an opening, is a lot of dust and dead air."

Nick reflected for a moment before responding. "Well, I got it to use ... and that's my need." He then asked the locksmith if maybe one of the other locksmiths at the shop might have better luck.

"No way," was the reply. "I'm the only person in the shop who works on safes, and probably the best on the island at what I do. That's why I'm giving you an accurate and professional assessment. Another locksmith who isn't as professional might just start drilling it and in the process not only *not* open it, but destroy whatever value it might have as well. Let me just say that this safe is going to be a monster to open. It looks like it has been locked for a long, long, time."

Sara looked at Nick knowing what he would now say.

"Thanks for the advice. I'll have to think about all this." Nick's voice was barely audible, but his disappointment couldn't be disguised.

"That'll be fifty dollars," the locksmith stated in a polite but determined manner.

"Fifty dollars?" questioned Nick.

"I won't charge for the appraisal, but it's fifty for the service call out here."

"Oh, thanks," Nick said. "Is a check okay?"

"You bet," was the reply.

As the sound of the locksmith's van faded down the road Nick looked at Sara and exclaimed, "Alex!"

"Alex Boreshanko?" asked Sara.

"Yes," Nick retorted. "He owes me big for a few stock tips I gave him, and I think he would *love* an island vacation out here for a few days."

New York

The warm, mild winds embraced the marina as spring struggled to change the Atlantic shoreline. Alex Boreshanko peered into the rearview mirror of his Jaguar and enjoyed the last glimpse of the New York City skyline. The Jaguar roared by, ignoring the "NO VEHICLES BEYOND THIS POINT" sign as it violated the dock planks, causing them to give up their clankity-clank sound to its wheels.

The car came to a stop next to an older but very impressive yacht. This was Alex's second home. With his safe and vault sales room in Manhattan it was a long ride to his Jersey Coast home, so Alex crashed here and called it his weekday residence. He preferred it to an apartment in town and he could use it as a tax write-off. Often he entertained clients on the yacht, and it afforded him a business advantage as well as enjoyment.

Alex was a bear of a man who seemed to embody a unique chemistry. He was a man full of life to whom people seemed instantly drawn. Alex always had a smile on his face and a spark in his eye. He was a powerful man—as powerful as Rasputin—but he also had the charm of the Dalai Lama. It would only fit then that this man's yacht was no toy. It had twin diesel screws and heads both fore and aft. When one was aboard and leaned over the side it seemed nosebleed high.

As Alex boarded his yacht his cell phone emitted a classical ringtone announcing a call. Flicking the phone to the open position, he did not hesitate to answer, knowing that only his closest of friends had this cell number.

"Yes?" answered Alex.

"Hey, you Ukrainian bear," was the response.

It was a voice from his past, calling from Vancouver Island.

After a few friendly insults "real men" seem to feel are needed in renewing a bonding, Nick asked Alex if he would like to come out to visit an old friend.

"Sara and I bought an old safe, and the local locksmith doesn't feel comfortable enough with it to attempt an opening."

"How is Sara?" Alex now interrupted.

"Oh, she's fine, Alex. We were both talking about you today. Sara was reminding me about the last time we got together on that yacht of yours. Boy, what a party you threw. Did that Russian couple ever open the jewelry store they talked about? They were sure interesting. I still can't believe the stories *he* told. That was a great time, Alex."

"Nick, what's this about a safe you guys bought?"

"It's a Chubb and has dual key operation."

"Nick, are you trying to scare me?" Alex's belly laugh could be heard clear across the wharf. "Does it have an isolator unit and a glass plate re-locker system?" he further joked.

"No, but it has boobs and long eyelashes," returned Nick.

Both men laughed, realizing how strong their friendship was.

"So ... what do you think, Alex?"

"It should be a hoot. I can't wait to get out there, Nick. I'll make the arrangements and get back to you."

Alex felt a chill run through him as he flicked his cell phone shut. It was unusual in that it was fairly warm out and he was dressed appropriately for the weather. Alex looked out over the moorage and mused about his anticipated vacation and reunion with Nick and Sara, his favorite couple.

Vancouver Island

Lording from its perch upon a topped cedar tree, an eagle with a laser stare adjusts its view by quickly jerking its head. Below, a figure flows across the red-wood sundeck as it voices the same words, over and over: "Step like a cat, flow like water, stand like the mountain...step like a cat, flow like water, stand like the mountain."

The end of this routine revealed a figure that was definitely more human than cat.

Nick had finished his Tai Chi practice for the morning.

Originally, Tai Chi gave Nick and Sara an opportunity to embrace the local culture. Sara had enjoyed the classes, but Tai Chi had developed into something more for Nick. His Qi energy level strengthened and he truly felt a renewed bond between himself, the universe, and Mother Earth. The martial arts aspect gave him a confidence that showed in his posture and everyday activities.

The breakfast area was only a few steps from the deck and offered the identical ocean view of the mainland's snow-capped Coastal Mountain Range. Today, the thirty miles separating their seaside cottage from the mainland of British Columbia seemed insignificant. Nick joined Sara for a good cup of coffee. Coffee was something Nick and Sara only indulged in on weekends or when traveling. Their weekday morning drink of choice was Chinese green tea. Somewhere Sara had read about the anti-oxidant benefits of green tea and it fit in with their newly minted healthy lifestyle. Not only was today a coffee treat day, but the beans were brewed on Salt Spring Island by a craft brewer.

Sara suddenly jumped backward as a wave of coffee spilled on the newspaper she had just been reading.

"Nick!" said Sara with alarm. There is a picture in today's *Daily News* of a building that burned down to the ground yesterday."

"Why are you so emotional about this, Sara? It can't be anything on the scale of when Chinatown burned down in 1960. That was so huge that it is still talked about to this day, and someone even wrote a play about it."

"But Nick, this building is the pawnshop we were in just a few days ago, where we bought the safe!"

"Give me a look, Sara!"

As Nick read the paper he bought into the excitement.

"That *is* the same store we purchased the safe at Sara. Holy jeez! Look at this—it states there was a fatality! Some young male who had only just worked there a short time … and the cause of the fire is unknown but suspicious."

"Nick," Sara spoke his name with slow deliberation, "do you suppose the safe we bought had anything to do with this?" Before Nick was able to respond, Sara followed with another question. "Nick, do you think we are in any kind of danger?"

"Well, first of all, Sara, no one knows who bought the safe. We were strangers and I paid in cash with no receipts. Also, there was no delivery involved."

"But what about the locksmith we had out here, Nick?"

"Sara, we never told him where the safe came from. Also, there isn't any mention of a safe in this article regarding the fire at the store.

"Do you think, Nick, that we should go to the police with this?"

"Not really, Sara. This is all speculation, and the safe probably has nothing to do with *any* of it."

"Nick, the locksmith did bring up the possibility of something being in the safe. Do you think there could be something valuable in it?"

"We really shouldn't let our imaginations go into overdrive, Sara."

"But Nick, this is *quite* a coincidence."

"Yes, and that's probably all it is. Alex will arrive tomorrow, and after he opens it, we will probably all have a good laugh at what we find."

"I hope so, Nick."

Unlocking The Past

The plane descended through misty clouds and Vancouver Airport was visible. An earlier temperate drizzle had set the scene: the gentle wetness was still warm with energy and only a fine mist remained of the rain.

Alex enjoyed his window seat. He viewed the runways and buildings as the large plane taxied the last several hundred feet. A few remaining raindrops on his porthole window created fragments of light that turned his attention from the view outside to the plane's interior.

The long trip from New York City had ended.

Alex followed the crowd to the baggage claim section, anxiously seeking some very special parcels he had put together. An aluminum box with exotic-looking fasteners was spotted in the mountain of luggage. Alex quickly lifted it from the conveyor. He spotted his second box—a very long box that sported a sticker with the word *Olympus*.

A young man to Alex's right was incessantly chewing gum all the while unconsciously bobbing his head. The cheeky lad looked at the long box and snickered, "What'cha got in the box? A rifle?"

Alex turned and gave him a smile, the kind of smile that betrays irritation. His eyes opened wider, causing the young man much uncertainty. "Very long-stemmed roses," answered Alex coolly.

"What?" The gum chewer stopped in mid-chew.

"The long box ..."

Alex's deep, loud laugh infected everyone nearby. People looked over at this laughing "Buddha." Everyone in the baggage area was now either smiling or laughing. Alex was that sort of man; he could scare the wits right out of you then a second later have you laughing like you hadn't since childhood.

Alex had acquired most of his experience with safes in Europe. He had cut his teeth on the likes of Chubb, John Tann, and Chatwood Milner. The last twenty years were spent working on American and Canadian safes, completing an impressive portfolio of challenges.

Armed with his equipment and expertise the man was unstoppable. If the safes and vaults in British Columbia were human, they would now be pleading with Alex to be spared. Alex had never encountered a safe he couldn't open and, in *most* cases, he'd never needed to use a drill—or any type of physical attack. He was the consummate manipulator and lock picker. Most often his entries could be classified as surreptitious. Even in the case of safe malfunctions, he was usually successful in using his manipulation skills to diagnose the problem and enable an opening.

"Hey, Alex," Nick called out as Sara waved.

The threesome embraced, chatting and laughing. A night ferry ride to Vancouver Island awaited the old friends as they embarked in high spirits.

Morning

"What a wonderful breakfast, Sara," said Alex as he dabbed with a wetted napkin some of the fresh strawberry juice he was now wearing on his tee shirt. "Those crepes were delicious and the scenery is more than breathtaking," he continued. Alex noticed the resident eagle atop a tall fir, then continued to scan over the arbutus trees to the granite outcroppings that formed little islands not far offshore. Across the sixty kilometers of the inside channel the snow-capped Coastal Mountain Range added the final majesty.

"Nick, I can't believe you and Sara get to see this every day."

"Yeah, you're preaching to the choir, Alex. Both Sara and I have been in love with British Columbia for many, many years."

The two men left the view from the deck behind as

they stepped into the bright room beyond the sliding glass doors. Nick pushed on the wall and a section of door opened to a room where the safe sat.

"Well, what do you think, Alex?" queried Nick.

"Oh, this is certainly a well-made safe," came the reply. "It's basically a Chubb coffer safe. I've never seen one exactly like this. It must have been specially made and limited in production. And having double key locks could double the difficulty of the opening."

"What does that all mean, Alex?"

Alex continued, with that kindness in his voice usually exhibited by a teacher who recognizes the sincerity of a question posed by a student: "Well Nick, this is no common safe, and it surely wasn't designed and constructed for the average person needing to protect his family photographs. These types were meant to hold precious stones, cash, or jewelry of some value. The barrier material making up the five sides and the door on this container leaves drilling only as an option of last resort."

"How do we open it then, Alex?"

"What do you mean *we*," chuckled Alex. "Don't you mean *me*?" Alex turned away with a follow-up smile on his face that usually meant he was enjoying it all.

The Chubb safe was of a typical European style that lacked any sort of combination lock dial. There was, instead, two keyholes surrounded and covered by heavy brass fobs, which slid upward. Only then were the keyways revealed.

Alex inserted his Olympus scope into the first keyhole. His eye followed the scope into the fully lighted opening; he focused intensely. The microsecond flickering of his eye ressembled a TV screen with no picture—just random, short-lived sparks of light dancing about. The safecracker's mind was now functioning like a computer, running programmed commands: first determining how many levers there were, then their shape, and if the lock model was identifiable. He was also searching to determine if the lock was of a key retaining design. He then probed inside the lock with a tool.

The same procedure was followed on the second lock.

"I can't take the suspense, Alex," Nick said nervously.

Alex looked at Nick and enlightened him: "Nick ... this safe is best opened by *listening* to it. You let it tell you what its secrets are. Opening a safe is a lot like seducing a woman; if you try to force your way and be rough, all you'll get is a lockout. You must invest some time and let her tell you about herself."

Alex paused to take a long sip of water before proceeding.

"The levers are lifting and dropping just as they should. I can tell you that the locks, so far, appear to be in good condition ... and I would say, in working order. Sometimes when these old safes are not used regularly, the levers can set up on you. When that happens, even the correct key might not operate."

Alex now lifted his "2 in 1" pick tool and held it in close proximity to his face. The shank of the pick tool appeared to be about ten inches long. At the end, was a fixed blade. A second blade was free to slide along the stem of the pick and was operated by a connecting handle.

"Since the levers are moving freely and have a good "feel," I should have good luck ... unless the false gateways fool me," said Alex. "But, again, that's where a woman and a safe are alike. That is, the more experience you have with either, the more likely you know how to get around problems and accomplish your mission."

Alex inserted his 2 in 1 pick and put slight turning pressure on the bolt-retracting piece. While doing this with his left hand, he now moved a second part of the pick that was free to slide along the stem of the tool, first toward himself, and then in a sideways motion.

For ten minutes this continued until the handle of the pick flopped over in a turning motion, producing the solid, heavy metal sound that old lock bolts make when they slam to the open position.

"One lock opened," Alex uttered with a controlled excitement driving his voice. "We are now on second base, Nick, with only the second lock keeping us from scoring."

With his 2 in 1 pick still protruding from the first keyhole, Alex produced another, identical pick, and carefully slipped it into the second lock's keyhole.

The minutes passed more quickly now that they smelled victory, and Nick and Alex proceeded with the confidence that only initial success can engender. As the second lock yielded with the now familiar and cherished slamming sound of a thrown bolt, the two men's eyes widened and their nostrils flared slightly. Now they were two pirates opening an imagined treasure chest and they felt the same excitement one feels when a life-changing event is anticipated.

Nick couldn't believe his eyes as Alex finally turned the L-shaped door handle. A slight tug on the handle sent the door gliding on its hinges. The hearts of both men stopped beating; neither drew a breath until the door finally opened a full ninety degrees.

Alex, in a display of his Ukrainian humor, and in an attempt to regain partial composure, looked at Nick and said, "Nick, here's still another way in which a safe is like a woman ... if you do everything right, *and* you're good, you'll get your way!"

Both men laughed so hard they momentarily forgot that the safe was now open and offered a clear view of its interior.

+++++++++++++

An old Beaver float plane was landing in the channel in front of Newcastle Island.

The plane passengers peered down at the crowded ferry terminal. Vehicles were boarding the ferry while a few walk-on passengers were still bidding their farewells in the parking lot.

"Thanks so much for everything, Alex. Are you sure you don't want to stay a few more days?" asked Nick.

"No, it was great seeing the both of you—and Vancouver Island—but my plane leaves tomorrow and there's an old Ukrainian buddy in Vancouver who would never forgive me if I didn't 'do the town' with him tonight." Alex now smiled at Nick and Sara, and with humor and fun in his voice said, "I'll protect you and Sara from such debauchery by going by myself," Alex's voice was full of high spirits and levity as the threesome laughed as one.

Nick and Sara returned to their car. Their attention and conversation now focused on the safe that had been opened just the previous day.

"I guess we should be happy that the safe is usable and that Alex was able to change some levers and make us new keys to operate it."

"Yeah," said Sara, "but since it wasn't in fact empty, you would think it could at least have a few coins in it—or even a nice piece of jewelry. I wonder why someone would protect something as small in value as a few books, a scroll that appears to be in Chinese and some old literature pertaining to a New Age society? I don't suppose the whole lot is worth five or six loonies."

"Well, Sara, maybe the two books *are* worth something. I can take them down to Fran at the Book Bank and see what she can tell me about them. Oh well, we do have a good safe for the house now. Have you heard any more about that fire at the pawnshop?"

"No, Nick, there hasn't really been anything more in the local paper. I guess it was nothing like we thought."

Twelve Karate Brother

The temperature was comfortable for a spring day. Sunshine was filling the air with a positive force. It was not too hot, but definitely short-sleeve weather. Nick and Sara were on their way to the Book Bank when Sara looked up from the sidewalk only to be pleasantly surprised.

"Carol, is that you," asked Sara?

"Sara? Oh, my goodness…it has to be twenty years," exclaimed Carol.

"Maybe more," said Sara.

"Nick … this is Carol Ming, an old friend of mine from high school. Carol, this is my husband, Nick."

Nick returned Carol's warm and polite smile.

Sara couldn't believe how well Carol had kept. Carol's skin was as smooth as a baby's and she betrayed no signs of aging. Sara remembered how exotic-looking and attractive her young Chinese friend had been when they were growing up together.

"Nick, did you know that Sara and I worked together at the Biological Station? It was our first job after high school," Carol said with an English accent.

Nick shook his head in response to Carol's question. He looked up at a totem pole behind the two women. He couldn't help but smile. On this one spot, three cultures seemed to be converging—English, Chinese and First Nations—a powerful, heady and timeless mix.

"Look, Sara, why don't you and Carol have a coffee or tea across the street while I take these two books to Fran?"

Within seconds the two women were like old friends again, chatting about girlhood times. Nothing else mattered as they crossed the street in a state of anxious anticipation that only a promised combination of coffee and good company can provide.

Nick made his way to the Book Bank thinking how lucky he was to have an attractive wife like Sara and how pleased he was that she had such a pleasant and attractive friend like Carol.

"Fran," I have a few books I've come across in my travels and wondered if you could tell me if they are of any consequence. That is, if you would be so kind?"

"Of course, Nick, I'd be delighted."

Less than ten seconds had passed when Fran looked up at Nick with excitement.

"Nick, how did you ever come by these?"

"Why, Fran … are they worth anything?"

"Your first book is *Unsigned Letters of a Brother* and the second is *The Three Truths*."

Nick's eyebrows raised, revealing his interest and excitement.

Fran continued. "Well, these were both written by Brother XII. Anything by him is extremely rare."

"Who is this *Brother XII*, Fran?"

"Where do I start? He was, you might say, a cult leader who lived in this area during the late 1920s and even into the early years of the 1930s. He had thousands of followers from all over the world and amassed what would be today many millions in property and gold. His involvement with other men's wives helped make him controversial. He also exercised absolute control over his followers. Being a practitioner of the occult enabled him to have an advantage over most people. Brother XII and his followers eventually had colonies at Cedar By The Sea, DeCourcy Island and Valdes Island. To this day, people are still digging up what used to be his commune of DeCourcy and Valdes Islands, searching for his gold stash."

"Whatever became of this Brother XII," asked Nick?

"There has been much speculation on just that question, but no one has ever proven conclusively what actually did become of him."

A silence swept over the room as Nick reflected on what had been said.

"Nick, do you have anything else besides these two books?"

"Yes, I have some pamphlets related to some group called the Aquarian Society and what is obviously an old scroll in Chinese or something."

"Nick, this is really amazing stuff!"

Fran's normally relaxed features now tightened, betraying a tension that was new to Nick.

"Nick, I think you should be warned that you could be into something dangerous. Not many people know this, but there have been the occasional rumors that members, who remained loyal to Brother XII, or to be more exact, descendants of this cult are still around and they do *not* want people snooping. This Chinese connection is something that no one knows about. I have learned of it, and I am telling you right now that maybe you should just entrust me with the items you have come by and I can sell them to an interested collector I know in England. You won't get rich off this, but it is worth in the thousands of dollars to him, I'm sure."

"Oh, Fran, I think I'll just keep these items and maybe do a little research on my own for entertainment."

"Nick, please don't let anyone know you have these things. It wouldn't be a good idea."

The power of Fran's warning was playing on Nick's mind as he crossed the street to collect Sara. Nick's posture stiffened as if suddenly armor-clad as the emotional stress affected his conscious mind. He wondered if there was any sort of intellectual or moral justification that would give him the green light to ignore Fran's caution and launch an investigation into this so-called Brother XII.

In the few minutes that Nick was in the Book Bank, what had been a beautiful spring day had transformed into a breezy, overcast one. A sudden, warm gust caused Nick's silky shirt collar to unravel as the sky opened up, releasing a downpour of rain. With a sense of paternal protection Nick quickly shoved the two "Brother Twelve" books into his multi-colored Hawaiian shirt. Nick hopped over the water, which was now pushing against the curb, unaware that the most valuable item the safe had yielded was not these tomes he was presently guarding, but the scroll with Chinese characters, now securely locked inside the Chubb safe.

Chinatown

The silky pure white beard of the old man, who sat alone in silence, offered the only strong contrast to the dark background of wooden bins, washed clean and worn smooth, some filled with dried herbs, others lending support for hanging bouquets of dried, muted flowers. Huang Ming was an accomplished master healer and a priest. Here, he prepared, sorted and stored his herbs. Master Ming, as he was known in Vancouver's Chinatown, was a scholar and a healer.

He was practicing his calligraphy as the chime, triggered by the opening door, announced the arrival of visitors. As his eyes gazed beyond the waterfall of bamboo and rock he observed an elegant, smartly dressed woman accompanied by a more casual, yet good-postured gentleman.

Nick and Sara had found their way through the seedy street of Hastings and into the heart of Vancouver's Chinatown.

"We're sorry," apologized Nick, but I thought the door we entered went into another hall. I never would have opened it if I knew it led directly to your residence. My name is Nick Konic and this is my wife, Sara. We are friends of your niece, Carol Ming."

The master merely nodded ... allowing Nick to continue.

"Sara and I are from Vancouver Island. We came over on the Harbour Lynx ferry."

A still and quieting presence filled the room.

"Carol told me of your coming, and of your request," Ming softly offered. "Do you bring the scroll of which she spoke?"

Nick produced the document he had stored in a cardboard tube—the type in which posters are shipped. The document unraveled, displaying a parchment quality associated with important printing. The old man's eyes explored the opened piece with controlled yet extremely attentive interest.

"This is very interesting. I'm not familiar with anything quite like this," he said non-committally.

"Can you tell us what it says," asked Sara?

"It is best described as a Saga," Ming stated. "It tells of a white man who is not white."

"Whatever does that mean," Sara begged?

"It also tells of this man obtaining a ship, in this case specifically, a Chinese junk ... in exchange for gold coins ... and leading what is left of his people out into the ... well, for lack of a better word ... what might be called a diaspora. There is mention of his setting out for the China Sea, but it also promises a return to the Holy Land someday. That is the gist of it. There is more, but only supporting detail, such as the place they left from, which is San Francisco. It is … a saga … a story of some religious group and their destiny."

"Is San Francisco the so-called Holy Land to which this group is to return" asked Nick?

Ming took more time to further study the scroll.

Finally, after exhaling a prolonged breath, he spoke again. "No," answered Master Ming, "that is clear enough. The so-called Holy Land is the place from which they were originally driven."

"And … where is that," asked Sara?

"It states that the Holy Land is a group of Islands somewhere far north of what is San Francisco."

"Is that all it says?" Nick felt compelled to ask.

"No," Master Ming informed them. "There is more detail, but part of this is written with the stylus, in ancestral form, while still other parts are *brush* writings. The characters will take time to translate fully. If you can leave this with me I will work on finishing the parts that are difficult to translate presently."

"Why yes, Master Ming. I would entrust you with this in the hope of a more complete reading at a later date, that is, if you would be so generous as to help us in this way."

"My niece's wish will be honored," promised Ming.

Nick and Sara returned Master Ming's courteous nod with a slight inclination of their shoulders before taking their leave of him.

Master Ming was still reading the scroll as the chime signaled the departure of Nick and Sara. As he unrolled the scroll for a more complete viewing, it separated, as if ripped, producing a smaller piece of scroll of exotic mathematical notations and algorithms.

Ming raised his head—he had heard a muffled, almost imperceptible, noise. He paused and stared in the direction of the hallway, his eyes seemingly capable of penetrating the wall. He quickly returned the scrolls to the tube-like holder, then hid it in a cubbyhole.

+++++++++++++

Island time could not slow down the approach of summer. Soon the swelling populations of tourists were crowding in like the tides. Vancouver Island became even more alive and a pulsation of energy defined the moment. The out-of-doors dominated Nick and Sara's attention and sea kayaking and hikes replaced the Book Bank and other downtown activities.

It had been weeks since their visit to Chinatown and they had still not heard from Master Ming. It seemed like years ago, not weeks, but the arrival of a new season has that kind of amnesiac power to paint one into a whole new frame. Nothing that had happened last season was dominating Nick and Sara's attention as much as the present. The scent of the summery ocean breeze found its way through the opened roof of the Lexus SC and the warmth of summer promised protection as it mingled with the rushing air, enhancing Nick and Sara's relaxing ride.

The hours passed, as did the day. The pearlized white car pulled into the Marina at Schooner Cove. Nick and Sara found their way to the closest dock and within moments each were in kayaks, paddling in unison.

A still surface was invaded by the blades of their paddles, which seemed to have a purpose greater than mere propulsion. The water was made to part then return to its previous flatness, first allowing the intruders to pass, then closing to remove any evidence of their presence.

Soon, the two kayaks were part of the horizon, swallowed by the enormity of the distant mountains and the flat sea. Nick and Sara were now experiencing one of those moments when nature reaches that other, deeper intelligence, permitting a non-verbal understanding of one's place in this world.

"What is that island, Nick?"

"Lasqueti," answered Nick. As a matter of fact, the part of Lasqueti that we face now, but is many kilometers away, is "Poor Man's Rock."

"What in the world is Poor Man's Rock?" laughed Sara.

"Oh, that's a name made famous by *Poor Man's Rock*, the book by Bertrand Sinclair."

"Who is this Sinclair guy, Nick, and how do you even know about *him*?"

"Well, one day when I was in the Book Bank, I purchased a book with the title *Poor Man's Rock*. I later asked Fran if she had ever read it. Fran filled me in on Sinclair and I read the story as well. Poor

Man's Rock is a reference to an area off Lasqueti Island," continued Nick. "The book is a great piece of romance written some eighty or more years ago, and it's still relevant today because of its understanding of the need for proper management regarding commercial fishing. It demonstrates, by its storyline, the risks to the environment from overfishing, and this can also be applied to forestry endeavors."

"But why" asked Sara, "is the book, as well as the area off Lasqueti, called Poor Man's Rock?"

"Well," Nick answered, "even though the large commercial seine boats overfished the other areas, leaving the poorer citizens without much fish stock, the rock just offshore from Lasqueti rose high, making a large section of the water in that area shallow. That meant commercial seine boats didn't enter there and the poorer people in their small rowboats could take advantage of this. Thus the name was given to this area," said Nick, who suddenly came to a realization. "Heidi-ho," he exclaimed as he used his paddle to send a thin curtain of water in the direction of Sara's kayak. "Do you know that I never did get back to Fran with this Brother XII business?"

"And Carol's uncle, Master Ming, has yet to get back to us regarding the scroll," added Sara.

"Yes, the summer has been slipping by and we haven't even realized it," Nick lamented. "We really should follow up on these things, Sara," he added with a sense of urgency. "After all, we certainly have the time."

They both fell silent and thoughtful. The natural peace around them had been disturbed, and what had been a relaxing afternoon was now charged with an air of anxiety.

"Nick, why are you getting so emotional? I also can't believe we have neglected this thing, but at least I've felt safe ... and it was comforting not thinking about that whole thing for a while."

Danger In the Air

This was not the same peaceful room in which they had first met Master Ming. The master had requested that his second meeting with Nick and Sara take place in a much smaller, darker room. Incense filled the room, adding an air of mysticism. Two Chinese men in martial arts garb were standing in the anteroom that Ming and the Konics had to pass through. Nick wanted to lighten the moment with some humor, but he did not want to risk being insolent. With measured words Nick asked Master Ming about the fearsome-looking guards.

"Those men are for our protection ... meaning you two especially," volunteered Ming.

"May I ask what additional information you have found, Master Ming?"

"There is not much different from what I have stated," replied Ming. "However, there is reason to believe, from what I have read, that this document itself is viewed as a most sacred object by the group it describes, if, in fact, they still exist today." Ming continued, "Whether the descendants of this group still exist or not I cannot say with certainty, but if they do, they would go to any measure to recover this document. It is, in essence, considered to be sacred by those who wrote it, and possibly others. I should also mention that along with this saga is a cryptographic mathematical piece that I cannot decipher. I have not the abilities from my alchemist background to translate this and have sent a portion of it to an old friend in China."

"Well," Nick now volunteered, "I don't think Sara and I need to take on any risk, and we certainly don't have any special need for this scroll. Is it something *you* would be interested in, Master Ming?"

"It is of no use to me," Ming answered, "but since you are friends of my niece I can hold it for you in safekeeping. This I offer, only because I have much protection, but you with this, might be as two sparrows surrounded by a room full of cats. I will keep it safe for you until you tell me otherwise."

"Sara and I are grateful to you, Master Ming. Thank you for the benefit of your wisdom and your protection."

"We are also in debt to your niece—and my friend— Carol Ming," added Sara.

"Go and seek wisdom; the day is already chasing at your heels," were Ming's parting words of advice to the now somewhat concerned couple.

++++++++++++

Having the use of their auto this time meant taking the Horseshoe Bay ferry back. The ferry attendant was fastening the snaps on the window curtains at both ends of the ship. Night was approaching, and the ride on the ferry seemed an especially long one for Nick and Sara. There was a rumble in the floor, as the ferry seemed to be struggling as it pushed through the water. Sara looked into Nick's eyes and asked him if he knew what they were getting into.

"I'm actually a little frightened," Sara shared with Nick. "Do you think any of those people could still be alive today?"

"I doubt if *they* are, but there could very well be descendants who have not only survived but still buy into the whole program. Well, I guess a trip to Fran Nielsen should be our next port of call," Nick concluded before turning to stare quietly out the side windows into the night.

++++++++++++

A heavenly filigree of stars danced their way through the skylight of the Konic's bedroom. Nick and Sara looked up, not finding the comfort they usually did in such celestial displays. Their bedtime conversation was evidence of their shared insomnia.

"Nick, I think someone was watching us on the ferry back from Vancouver tonight."

"I don't want to worry you, Sara, but when I drove

the last mile or two coming home ... a car seemed to be following us," rejoined Nick.

"Nick, what are we getting into? I think the things that came out of that safe are very powerful ... and may be more than we want to be involved with."

"Sara, I think what we need more than anything now is to have more information so we can better judge and understand what we are becoming a party to."

"How do we do that, Nick?"

"Well ... the most knowledgeable person regarding this area and local history seems to be Fran."

"Fran ... at the Book Bank?" queried Sara. "How do we know we can trust her?"

"We don't. But who do you suggest we go to with this story of coincidences and what would seem to others as vivid imaginations?"

"Imaginations! I don't think we are imagining this, Nick! And what about Ming? He thinks we are into something dangerous. Ming could just explain this all to the local police and we could dissociate ourselves from this scary thing."

"Sara, I don't think Ming will cooperate with the police on this one. He is doing *us* a favor, but the Chinese are a society unto themselves here. They have been outsiders for over a hundred years and, in their wisdom, have survived. The Canadian Chinese are model citizens, but people like Ming know how they have been treated. They were always paid less and given the *absolutely* most dangerous jobs in the coal mines of this area. That is well documented. They helped build the railroads in B.C. and again were given the most dangerous jobs for the least money. And don't forget, during the Second World War other Asians, the Japanese, were put into internment camps and, in many cases, had their possessions and wealth confiscated. Even though the Chinese are as much Canadian as any other group, many still consider themselves outsiders."

"Nick, that's true of *all* groups," said Sara.

"You think so?"

"You bet! Jews, French, First Nations peoples, Blacks, Japanese, Muslims ... and so on, only when they intermarry do they seem to create a new entity that becomes Canadian."

"Sara, aren't you forgetting the cultural mosaic? They can still be these things and be Canadian at the same time. For example, Indo-Canadian, French-Canadian ..."

"Oh, you mean a hyphenated Canadian?"

"Yeah ... well, I guess so." Nick paused. "Maybe you're right, Sara, but Ming will still be careful about what he claims. The story sounds shaky enough coming from us. Let's not go there, Sara."

+++++++++++++

It was upon Fran's insistence that she meet Sara and Nick after hours in the privacy of the rare book room. The usual, pleasant music complimented the ornate rugs and very special bookbindings that lined the walls.

"I knew you would be returning with questions, and perhaps some fear," opened Fran.

"To say the least!" Nick replied "These past few days have been somewhat unnerving for Sara and me."

"From what you have told me on the phone," said Fran, "I think your journey has already begun and the option of 'opting out' is no longer yours."

"You seem to know a lot about this whole thing, Fran. Can you help us see more clearly what is going on here?"

"I can tell you all I know, but there is another who will be able to make this all come together for you."

"Who is he—or she?" asked Sara.

"Well, first you must understand that what I am about to tell you is not proven fact, but only my understanding of events. In the 1920s there was a cult leader in British Columbia who went by the name "The Brother XII." He had a daughter he did not claim because he felt a female could never be his heir and the promised messiah. Not only was she a female but an illegitimate child as well. I will get back to her. Brother XII was good at faking things and creating illusions. He had sailed the Orient and learned secrets that gave him power over others who lacked such exposure. He came to this area and established a group … some would call it a cult. Brother XII eventually got into trouble with the law and after a lengthy trial soon fled, taking his gold and destroying what was left of his commune. I am of the understanding that he faked his death in Switzerland and took his mistress, Madame Zee, and a group of his followers to China.

"Who was this Madame Zee?" asked Sara.

"Madame Zee was described by many as a mean person who, some think, even controlled Brother XII. During the 1950s, there was a sighting in Nanaimo of a woman dressed entirely in black and who appeared to be from another period in time—a very stern-looking, some thought, scary woman."

"Yes!" Sara gasped. "What became of her?"

"She was only seen that one time. No one knows."

"So what happened to this Brother XII and Madame Zee when they got to China?" asked Nick.

"What happened there, I don't know, but the daughter I mentioned to you told me that she had seen her father in the early 1950s, some time after he returned from his China voyage. She is the only one who may be able to answer your questions."

"What is her name?" asked Sara with an eagerness that grew by the second.

"She goes by the name—"

Just then one of the books on the shelf plopped over on its side, startling everyone.

"—she calls herself Hetty, just Hetty."

"And where can one find this Hetty?" Nick inquired.

"She is a recluse, in an area near Kelsey Bay, not far from the First Nations' Lands. It is said that the First Nations believe she has special powers, and they are very protective of her. I can give you no more information than to say look in the area of Kelsey Bay. She will find *you* if she so wishes. There is only one more thing ..."

"What in God's name is it?" blurted Sara.

"Well … I don't want to overdramatize this, but you *do* realize that certain people may become dangerous if they perceive you as any sort of threat to their beliefs?"

Nick looked up with budding confidence, "It's like you said, Fran, our journey has already begun, and there is no opting out."

The Journey Begins

As the fully fueled Lexus left Schooner Cove the next day, Nick and Sara were both tingling with exhilaration befitting their new adventure. The fear they had experienced earlier was now replaced by a fresh confidence—no doubt reinforced by a buzz from the Tim Hortons coffees that they had picked up in Parksville. On the car sound system a CD of Roy Orbison's "Running Scared" was feeding their emotions with new bravado. They were anything *but* running scared. They were on their first real adventure and the world had better look out!

"Nick," Sara drawled, "how much did you tell Fran on the phone before we met with her?"

"Just that we had a translation of the scroll and that it mentioned an Exodus to China. I didn't mention Master Ming by name or any details involving him. That's all I told her."

Nick and Sara had been on the road to Kelsey Bay for over an hour and had made more than one coffee stop. Two half-empty paper cups were stained from overspills caused by lane changes and fast driving. The name *Tim Hortons* was barely legible on Nick's cup. Nick enjoyed running the car a little hard once in a while and appreciated its smooth handling. He never exceeded what he considered safe driving nor did he fancy extreme sports. However, driving to the fullest made him feel one with the road and that was a thrill he loved.

"Boy, when we get back on a regular schedule," said Nick, "I have to revisit green tea and get off this coffee binge. This stuff tastes good, but I think I'm overdoing it."

"That goes for both of us, Nick."

Nick and Sara left the Island Highway at the Campbell River exit. A short stretch of road soon connected them with the old highway and the panorama opened to a view of the ocean. Nick had more than the average attachment to his white convertible, but never more than when he and Sara drove along the ocean feeling the sea air and breathing the scent now so familiar to both of them.

"I think the ocean is the only remaining way to feel a sense of frontier," Nick mused as he momentarily looked over at Sara.

"Boy … Tai Chi man, you're getting philosophical."

"What's this 'Tai Chi man' stuff," Sara?

"Oh, I just think that since you've been studying Tai Chi you've gotten more and more reflective or something."

"So now it's your turn, Sara. Tell me something about this town we're now in."

"Well … Campbell River is a seaside town where the big fir and cedar trees meet the ocean and civilization. It got a reputation of sorts from years earlier when it was a summer stop frequented by not only Bing Crosby but by John Wayne, in his ship *The Wild Goose*. For years John Wayne use to make places like Campbell River, Nanaimo and Port Alberni part of his summer pilgrimage, and there are still a few people who can spin the many stories about the Duke. But that was in the past and no such notoriety surrounds Campbell River today, except for the occasional rumor that some American movie star bought a property on Quadra Island or some other nearby place."

Nick looked up to notice the traffic sign displaying options for faraway places and noticed they were leaving Campbell River.

"What now, Sara?"

"Well, Nick, for the remainder of the day, our only companions will be trees and highway. Once there, we'll *still* not be near a town of any consequence. At one time Kelsey Bay was the end of the Trans-Canada highway. Now the highway extends to Port Hardy, making Kelsey Bay only an outpost to be appreciated by those who seek wilderness and nature."

Sara ended her travelogue at that point so that she and Nick could enjoy the beauty around them in peaceful silence.

The Inn

November is the beginning of the rainy season on Vancouver Island and the further up-island a person ventures, the more it ressembles a rain forest. Nick and Sara had not seen a downpour for a long time, and they welcomed it as if they were accepting the change of seasons. When a new season arrives, it is always magical for the first day as it presents a freshness … after that … it is judged on its own merits.

A warm, wet, intermittent wind was in control of the faded sign, which was maintaining a sort of irregular back and forth movement, testing the rusty pins suspending it and allowing a poorly aimed, old floodlight to illuminate it at brief intervals, revealing, now and then, the word *Inn*.

"Heidi-ho, Sara, there's an Inn," said Nick removing his foot from the gas pedal.

"Nick, are you meaning that we should stay there for the night?"

"Well, Sara, it's the first sign of civilization we've seen in almost an hour and it *is* night," Nick said with an air of practicality.

"Nick, this place looks eerie, but I agree with you. I need a good meal and I am ready for some sleep."

Nick pulled up to the front, not far from the sign. Their car was the only vehicle in the lot.

As the couple passed through the front door they entered a large room where two men were playing a game of pool. Just down from the pool table there was a shuffleboard area, over which a bare lightbulb topped by a green tin shade cast its glow. To the left, there was a bar, and through a large, open doorway what appeared to be a dining area was visible.

Nick and Sara headed warily for the bar. They were greeted by a face whose smirk revealed a broken front tooth and whose two-day growth of beard couldn't hide a long scar. The couple were duly apprehensive.

"Is the dining room open?" Nick dropped his voice as deep as he could muster without making it sound forced and phony.

"This time of year there ain't many people who come up here, but it would not be a problem to tend to the kitchen. It would be a limited menu though."

A sense of relief surged through Sara as she realized that the bartender was more civil than his appearance would have her believe.

"You can have anything to eat—as long as it's fish and chips," offered the bartender in his new role of cook.

"Oh, that would be just fine," Nick said, knowing that, luckily, fish and chips happened to be one of Sara's favorite dishes.

"Eric," said the bartender-cook.

"What?" asked Nick.

"You can call me Eric."

"Why, yes. Eric. This is my wife, Sara, and my name is Nick. The sign outside says this is an Inn. Does that mean you have rooms to let?"

"Not a problem. It can be arranged," was Eric's accommodating response.

Sara and Nick enjoyed the meal—well beyond their expectations. The ample portions of halibut were surprisingly very fresh.

Sara finished her last sip of wine and Nick was not far behind with his pint of ale.

"I think I'll pass on dessert, Nick," she said sleepily.

In short order the arrangements for a room were made and Nick was handed a rather large bit key with a tag attached.

"Thank you, Eric," said Nick.

"You and the Mrs. have a good sleep," Eric replied.

"Say, Eric … would you happen to know a woman up here who goes by the name Hetty?" asked Nick.

A look of fear followed by anger caused Eric's eyes to bulge as he shook his head. He swallowed hard before speaking. "Why do you ask me about this Hetty?"

Nick and Sara looked at each other in silence.

Eric continued, "I am not from this area, but there is a popular legend I have heard the locals mention. It's about a witch named Hetty who lives in the deep forest. It is said she knows things humans could not possibly know. I think it's all fiction and she doesn't even exist … yes, it's just a fairy tale, a legend … whatever. Like Sasquash, she doesn't really exist and you're wasting your time even talking about such nonsense."

"Thanks, Eric. I guess you're right. We'd better turn in. Thanks again."

The age of the building was evident by the creaky wooden steps and the heavy old iron key that was supplied for their room.

"This is it, honey … No. 3."

"Nick," Sara now had a scolding tone to her voice. "I don't think it was wise of you to ask Eric if he knew anyone by the name of Hetty." Did you notice his reaction?"

"Yeah," said Nick, "he seemed a little too disturbed about something he says doesn't exist."

Nick unlocked the door and pushed into the room through what seemed to be very stale air lacking *any* sort of freshness.

"Nick … this place is creepy."

"Well, as long as it's clean, honey, we can ignore the atmosphere for now."

The room was finished with interlocking cedar planks that lined the walls and ceiling, giving it a solid, well-built feel. A large painting could be seen over the bed—it was an oil painting of a woman. Sara thought the painting had an Emily Carr quality, primitive yet not primitive. Far removed from the ocean scenes of Schooner Cove, this scene was typical of the forest area of Kelsey Bay, depicting a heavily forested cathedral of trees with great swirls of green. Completely incongruous, however, was the fact that the woman in the painting was dressed entirely in black—her formal attire did not fit the natural forest scene surrounding her.

As Sara stared at the painting something started to look more and more familiar. At last it registered with Sara. This was the same redheaded woman whose face she had seen while waiting for Nick to load the safe at the pawnshop. Yes! Sara remembered the woman dressed in black that she had momentarily seen that day; she had an identical face and the piercing eyes were an exact match. But had this woman been real or was she just an apparition?

Before Sara could even mention this amazing coincidence to Nick, she was overcome by what could best be described as a type of narcolepsy.

"Nick ... I feel really tired ... and my vision seems blurry. You don't suppose ... that the innkeeper slipped something ... into our drinks, do you?"

"Sara, you're being overly dramatic. I think you're just tired, like I am. Let's get some sleep. This day has been long. We are in a remote place and the weather doesn't help. I think we are both just overtired."

"Good night, dear," Sara slurred her words as she fell on the bed, sound asleep within seconds and still in her clothes.

"Honey ... wake up."

Although Nick gently moved Sara's shoulder backward and forward he couldn't bring her to. Nick noticed how attractive Sara still was. There is a special freshness to the skin when someone is asleep. All stress is gone and this relaxed state was becoming to his wife. Nick recalled their first encounter at that quaint sidewalk café in Amsterdam. He remembered how much Sara looked like a model; she carried herself with such class. He recalled his first trip to British Columbia with her—and all those summers. All those rides on the ferries with breathtaking vistas were always shared with Sara. Nick thought for a moment about how lucky he was to have found his perfect match. They always had fun together, no matter what they did. They were a team—inseparable.

Suddenly, Nick was quite overcome by tiredness too. Oh well, I might as well turn in, he thought. As he locked the door with the old key, he returned to the bed and gave Sara a good night kiss on her forehead.

"Good night, dear," he mumbled, almost collapsing on the bed.

+++++++++++++

The next morning was a welcomed dry day. Both Nick and Sara had overslept and were soon downstairs to inquire about a morning meal.

"I'll be right back, Sara, I'm going to throw our overnight bags into the car."

"That sounds good."

Sara could see into the adjoining room and noticed an oil painting on the wall. It was a portrait of a man standing before a group of people. The man had a goatee and very beady eyes. The painting seemed to glow so the image of the man seemed to stand out even in the somewhat dark room. Sara was mesmerized by the painting when suddenly someone touched her on the right shoulder causing her to jump back like a startled horse responding to a car horn.

"I hope I didn't scare you," said Eric.

"Oh, God!" said Sara. "You sure did."

"Will you and Mr. Konic be wanting breakfast this morning?"

"Why ... yes, that would be nice."

"Could I ask you a question?" said Sara.

"Sure."

"Who is the woman in the painting in Room 3, where we stayed?"

"I don't know, but I could ask the owner and find out for you."

"Oh, thank you, that would be appreciated, Eric."

After a quick "logger's breakfast" they were under way with their small overnight bags in the trunk of the car and each with a cup of coffee in their hands.

As Nick and Sara started to pull out, Eric stepped in front of the car, blocking their exit.

"Nick cautiously rolled down the window halfway while Eric walked around to the driver's door.

"Madame Zee," Eric said quietly as he placed his head within inches of Nick's.

"What?" asked Nick, somewhat confused.

Eric's voice was barely audible.

"The lady in the painting your wife asked about earlier ... her name is Madame Zee."

"Oh! Thank you, Eric," said Sara appreciatively.

The Holy Grail

Nick and Sara had only been driving a short time when they saw what appeared to be a broken-down pickup. The truck was an old Dodge that could have passed for some sort of hippie wagon from that time period referred to only as "the 60s." The hood was up, indicating a problem.

"Should I stop and offer help?" Nick asked Sara.

"I think it would be the right thing to do, Nick."

As the couple cruised up to the sad excuse for a pick-up truck, Nick could only see a single elderly woman whose appearance didn't match her age. She was standing in front of the truck, staring under the hood.

What an artsy type, Nick thought, suppressing a chuckle.

A burning cigarette extended from the pretentious-looking holder clenched between her lips. Her dress consisted of skintight leggings, commonly known in the 60s as "leotards." Her halter top was held up by an ample bosom that was complimented by a slender waist. Her white hair was pulled straight back off her face so that her profile was only interrupted by the protruding cigarette holder. She was truly a refugee from some 1960s art colony.

"Is there anything we could do to help?" asked Nick as he approached the eccentric-looking woman. Nick noticed that her old Dodge pickup had a generous smattering of "artwork" across it, the type usually associated with VW microbuses and hippies.

"Well, I could use a ride," the woman rasped in a deep, throaty voice, the cigarette holder bobbing up and down. "Can you take me to the nearest Petro station?" she asked, squinting through a puff of smoke while eyeing the tiny back seat of the SC Lexus.

"You bet," replied Nick. "Not a problem, except that our back seat ... if you could call it that ... is a real challenge for a fit."

The aging hippie accepted the ride.

As the threesome sped off they seemed to be on a mission, but it wasn't long before they were casually conversing about the area of Kelsey Bay and life in general. Easily ten minutes had passed before Nick realized that he and Sara hadn't properly introduced themselves.

"My name is Nick and this is my wife, Sara," volunteered Nick.

"I know. How do you do, Nick. Hello, Sara ... my name is Hetty."

Nick jerked his head back to peer into the rearview

mirror, focusing fully on their new passenger. He went silent for a moment before managing a response.

"So *you* are Hetty!"

Sara was as surprised as Nick. She didn't know what she had expected Hetty to look like, but this was *not* what she had envisioned.

Nick wondered how to tell Hetty that she was the object of their search. But he didn't have to.

"Hetty," Nick began—"

"I know," answered Hetty.

"You do?" asked Sara.

"You don't think that truck of mine had *really* broken down, do you? I had received word from a mutual acquaintance that you two were heading up here hoping to gain some answers to questions regarding my father, known as The Brother XII."

"Well ... yes," answered Sara with hesitation.

"Turn at the next dirt road on your right," Hetty ordered in an assuming fashion.

The car made a scraping noise as it started down the turnoff.

"This car is sort of out of place on a logging road, Hetty. I don't think I can take this rough road too far down."

"This is fine," ordered Hetty. Stop here and follow me."

Nick and Sara were led down what had now turned into a footpath. They were in some seriously remote forest area, but both Nick and Sara were confident because they felt—or at least hoped— that Hetty was trustworthy.

As they followed the footpath they could hear flute music, the deeply melodic kind of flute music made only by cedar flutes carved in the First Nation's style. Nick and Sara wondered if they were being lulled into some sort of trance as they stepped through an opening in the trees and saw before them several First Nations people. Their facial features and skin tone were easily recognizable. Nick had dealt with some tribe members when he used to buy fish with Sara's brother. They had made many trips to the Port Alberni Reservation. He didn't know how friendly this group would be to outsiders, but he was somewhat confident that Hetty was not leading them into serious trouble. Sara, on the other hand, was becoming very frightened, but she knew that Nick would not be continuing to follow Hetty if he felt this to be dangerous. She trusted his judgement; and besides, they really had no alternative at this point.

Several people stared at the two outsiders as they were led by Hetty into what appeared to be a half-finished house. The building looked like a typical raised ranch design except that it lacked windows, doors, and siding. As the couple entered, they noticed the dirt floors.

Hetty turned and looked at Nick and Sara in what seemed to be a cold and detached manner, bluntly asking them, "What do you know about The Brother XII and his society?"

Nick and Sara were now shaken and nervous. Outside were at least a dozen plenty big and unfamiliar men about whom Nick and Sara knew nothing; they were unlike anyone they had ever known.

Nick spoke up first, opting to level with Hetty because Fran might have already told her everything that had transpired between her and the Konics. After about five long minutes of background on themselves, Nick and Sara were finished. Now they both wondered if Hetty was someone who would, in turn, share her story with them and fill in the missing pieces.

Hetty spoke at last.

"I am only sharing this with you because you are already heavily involved, probably more than you even know, and because Fran is a dear friend whose judgement in people is always accurate. I am the out-of-wedlock daughter of The Brother XII. The Brother XII thought a daughter could never be a messiah. He felt his destiny had somehow been denied, and only later in life recognized, albeit in private, that I was his daughter."

Sara asked, "Does the society still exist today?"

"I have seen evidence of it. Although I am not a member myself, I have had people who claim to be active members come to me in hope of recruiting. I have no desire to become involved, but they are out there."

Sara cleared her voice and spoke up. "Had your father mentioned the Far East, mainly China?"

"First of all, my father is no longer alive. Enough said about that. It will remain private and personal. I must have something for myself. Yes, after he faked his death in Switzerland he fled to China with some followers. Some followers I talked to have spoken of a formula he unearthed in China. He was able to hide and protect this from the Japanese during the invasion."

"What is this formula about," asked Nick?

"I don't know exactly, but my father told me that he had found something that could change the power on the planet. He was talking about a paradigm shift that was mind-boggling."

"You see, The Brother XII and his group really came about because of the disappointment in mankind following World War I. People never wanted to repeat such a thing. The elimination of all future wars and the evil mindset associated with such violence was what their group was striving for. They sought to remove themselves from the evil elements in an insane world and searched for sanity instead. Most thought they could actually change the world … others were just satisfied to save themselves from what seemed the shortcomings of mankind and its imminent destruction."

Nick went on to plead for more information regarding the formula. "Did your father say anything more about the formula?" he asked.

"You know," said Hetty, "I heard the term 'reverse electrolysis' with some babble involving hydrogen. At the time it meant nothing, but now with all the news from Vancouver about fuel cells, I'm not so sure."

"The fuel cell was invented by Sir William Grove in the mid 1800s," Nick stated. "They've known about them for over one hundred years. Could it be that the formula is a way to make hydrogen for the fuel cells?" he mused.

"My father *did* mention that the Occident was going about everything in the wrong way."

"What does that mean?" asked Nick.

"Well, he said that the West views the world as a machine and man's role as that of mechanic, whereas the Chinese view the world as a living garden and that humankind should be gardeners … not mechanics."

"You're still losing me," Nick interrupted.

"Nick, the secret of the formula can only be released by a 'gardener' not a 'mechanic.' For example, a fish has the perfect membrane for splitting hydrogen off water to get its oxygen. It's called a gill. Yes, Nick, a gill holds the magic to membrane construction. And so does the leaf from a tree. The secret of the magic membrane for producing the needed ingredients for the Hydrogen Age can only be found by a *gardener* who understands nature—not a machine builder."

"So how is it done? What is the secret?" asked Nick, knowing that this was not something Hetty would likely share.

"Nick, my father told me that in China, over a hundred years ago, a formula had been discovered that held the key to everything I've mentioned to you. I have never seen any such thing and do not know for certain that it, in fact, exists."

Nick and Sara were obviously affected by all this information.

Hetty continued. "I think the group that follows my father today is more concerned about this formula in and of itself and have lost their devotion to the original ideals and goals of the founders," said Hetty. "Nick … Sara, I am sorry that you are a part of this now. Whether this formula exists, or if it even works, is only secondary. The danger is in the perception of certain people. Some members of what has become of The Brother XII's organization are seeking this rumored formula for peaceful reasons. They believe the story and want to make a better world. Others ... well ... they want only power, and will stop at nothing to get it."

"I guess the search for the Holy Grail never ends," Nick uttered as his voice dropped.

"Thank you, Hetty," Sara sighed, feeling deflated.

Hetty now looked up at Nick and Sara with heavy, tired eyes and said, "Take some advice from an old lady—you two just enjoy yourselves and forget about all this. There are people still searching for his millions in gold that were never accounted for, and others for some Holy Grail formula. None of it matters."

"But Hetty, do you think the formula does in fact exist?"

"Nick, I don't really know, and I may be wrong regarding what it involves. It might be about something totally different, but I *do* know my father said that what he had found was beyond anything man has yet known. It's a slippery slope we are talking about and a fall could be fatal. Please follow the advice of an old lady and protect yourselves by just forgetting you ever heard any of this."

"Do you think that's possible?" asked Sara with sincerity.

+++++++++++++++++

As Nick and Sara followed the road into Parksville after their encounter with Hetty, Nick wondered why they hadn't asked Hetty about the gold. Perhaps it would have portrayed them as gold seekers and discredit them in her eyes. But Nick couldn't help wonder if that gold had been deployed and what businesses or organizations today might be owned and run by its seed money.

"Oh, Nick," said Sara, "I forgot to ask Hetty about that woman I keep seeing! The one with the red hair who looks so eerie."

Nick looked over at Sara and said, "I think you and I are thinking the same thing."

"Is it what our Tai Chi instructor used to say, Nick?"

"Yeah, like he used to say, 'It doesn't matter ... it *just doesn't* matter.' "

"You're right, Nick. It *doesn't* matter. Let's just forget all this stuff and enjoy our retirement on this beautiful island—the Canadian Riviera."

"Do you really think we will be able to?"

"Let's hope so, Nick. I know one thing for sure. *We* won't go looking for *it* so maybe *it* will forget about *us*."

The dying rays of the sun shimmered faintly on the pearlized white convertible as Nick leisurely took a curve. The couple settled back into their seats for a relaxing journey—homeward bound. They gazed contentedly at the splendour of the sun setting on the snow-capped mountains, joining the sea to the sky, and their only wish at the moment was to return to their *safe, normal* lives.

But, after all, what *is* normal for Nick and Sara Konic on Vancouver Island?